Friend of the
Cathedral City Library
Donor
Cheryl Dawson-Voight
in honor of
Carrie and Laura Voight

® DEMCO, INC. 1989 PRINTED IN U.S.A.

P R E S E N T S

THE AMERICAN GIRLS
COLLECTION®

MEET FELICITY · An American Girl
FELICITY LEARNS A LESSON · A School Story
FELICITY'S SURPRISE · A Christmas Story
HAPPY BIRTHDAY, FELICITY! · A Springtime Story
FELICITY SAVES THE DAY · A Summer Story
CHANGES FOR FELICITY· A Winter Story

1774

MEET KIRSTEN · An American Girl
KIRSTEN LEARNS A LESSON · A School Story
KIRSTEN'S SURPRISE · A Christmas Story
HAPPY BIRTHDAY, KIRSTEN! · A Springtime Story
KIRSTEN SAVES THE DAY · A Summer Story
CHANGES FOR KIRSTEN · A Winter Story

1854

MEET SAMANTHA · An American Girl
SAMANTHA LEARNS A LESSON · A School Story
SAMANTHA'S SURPRISE · A Christmas Story
HAPPY BIRTHDAY, SAMANTHA! · A Springtime Story
SAMANTHA SAVES THE DAY · A Summer Story
CHANGES FOR SAMANTHA · A Winter Story

1904

MEET MOLLY · An American Girl
MOLLY LEARNS A LESSON · A School Story
MOLLY'S SURPRISE · A Christmas Story
HAPPY BIRTHDAY, MOLLY! · A Springtime Story
MOLLY SAVES THE DAY · A Summer Story
CHANGES FOR MOLLY · A Winter Story

1944

CHANGES FOR
FELICITY
A WINTER STORY

BY VALERIE TRIPP

ILLUSTRATIONS DAN ANDREASEN

VIGNETTES LUANN ROBERTS, KEITH SKEEN

PLEASANT COMPANY

PICTURE CREDITS
The following individuals and organizations have generously given
permission to reprint illustrations contained in "Looking Back":
pp. 64-65—*The Battle of Lexington,* The Granger Collection, New York; Courtesy
Library of Congress (snake); Colonial Williamsburg Foundation; pp. 66-67—
Wethersfield Historical Society, Wethersfield, Connecticut; AP/Wide World Photos;
Courtesy, American Antiquarian Society; Colonial Williamsburg Foundation
(gunpowder horn); pp. 68-69—Colonial Williamsburg Foundation; *Mitre Tavern,* The
Granger Collection, New York; Naval Historical Center, Washington, D.C.

Edited by Roberta Johnson
Designed by Myland McRevey and Michael Victor
Art Directed by Kathleen A. Brown

Library of Congress Cataloging-in-Publication Data

Tripp, Valerie, 1951-
Changes for Felicity : a winter story / by Valerie Tripp ; illustrations, Dan
Andreasen. — 1st ed.
p. cm. — (American girls collection)
Summary: The outbreak of the Revolutionary War in 1775 brings drastic
changes to Felicity's life in Williamsburg, affecting both her family and her
friendship with Elizabeth.

ISBN 1-56247-038-8 — ISBN 1-56247-037-X (pbk.)
1. United States—History—Revolution, 1775-1783—Juvenile fiction.
[1. United States—History—Revolution, 1775-1783—Fiction.
2. Williamsburg (Va.)—Fiction. 3. Friendship—Fiction.]
I. Andreasen, Dan, ill. II. Title. III. Series.
PZ7.T7363Cg 1992 [Fic]—dc20 92-12889 CIP AC

TO MY HUSBAND, MICHAEL
AND
MY DAUGHTER, KATHERINE
WITH LOVE

TABLE OF CONTENTS

FELICITY'S FAMILY

FATHER
*Felicity's father,
who owns one of the
general stores in
Williamsburg.*

FELICITY
*A spunky, spritely
colonial girl,
growing up just
before the American
Revolution in 1774.*

MOTHER
*Felicity's mother,
who takes care of
her family with love
and pride.*

NAN
*Felicity's sweet and
sensible sister, who
is seven years old.*

POLLY
*Felicity's baby sister,
the newest Merriman,
who was born in
December 1775.*

WILLIAM
*Felicity's three-year-old
brother, who likes mischief
and mud puddles.*

ELIZABETH COLE
Felicity's best friend,
who faces changes in
her family's life with
courage and hope.

GRANDFATHER
Felicity's generous
grandfather, who
understands what is
important.

PENNY
The spirited,
independent horse
Felicity loves.

BEN DAVIDSON
A quiet apprentice living with
the Merrimans while learning
to work in Father's store.

JIGGY NYE
Felicity's old enemy,
who treated Penny
cruelly.

A CARDINAL AND
A BLUEBIRD

"Would you like another tart?" asked
Felicity Merriman. It was a bright January
afternoon. Felicity and her best friend,
Elizabeth Cole, were playing with their dolls in the
Merrimans' sunny garden.

"Yes, thank you, Miss Merriman," said
Elizabeth politely. She took two of the brown twigs
Felicity offered her, one for herself and one for her
doll Charlotte. "You do make the most elegantly
delicious tarts."

"That's kind of you to say, Miss Cole," said
Felicity with a grin. "But I'm afraid these tarts are
overdone." She snapped a twig in two with a *crack*.

"I like crisp tarts," laughed Elizabeth, "and so

does Charlotte."

"Upon my word!" said a voice. The girls looked up and saw Felicity's grandfather standing at the garden fence. "It is Felicity in her red cloak and Elizabeth in her blue cloak. I thought you two young ladies were a cardinal and a bluebird perched on that garden bench. What a pleasant sight to see!"

"Grandfather!" called Felicity. She and Elizabeth gathered up their dolls and hurried over to him.

"Good day, sir," said Elizabeth. She made a little curtsy.

Grandfather bowed. "Good day, Elizabeth," he said. He nodded at the dolls. "Will you ladies do me the honor of introducing me to your friends?"

The girls looked at each other and giggled. "Oh, Grandfather," said Felicity. "You remember my doll, Susannah Maria Augusta Eliza Lucy Louise."

"Ah, yes, indeed," said Grandfather. "But somehow I can never remember her name. That is, I can't remember *all* of her name."

"My doll's name is Charlotte," said Elizabeth.

"Charlotte!" said Grandfather. "Is she named after Queen Charlotte, the wife of King George, ruler of England and all the colonies?"

"Yes," said Elizabeth.

"Then this is indeed an honor," said Grandfather. "She is loyal to the king. There aren't many of us Loyalists left. Some are in jail, some have fled to England, and

King George and
Queen Charlotte

some have changed their minds and become Patriots." He looked at Elizabeth sadly. "Your family and I are among the last Loyalists."

"Aye, sir," said Elizabeth.

Felicity was quiet. Her father supported the Patriots. So did Ben, his apprentice. They didn't think the king should rule the colonies anymore.

"Well!" said Grandfather briskly. "It's too sunny today to talk about cloudy subjects. I've been in Williamsburg for three weeks. It's been rainy and I've had a cold ever since I arrived. This is the first day I've been able to be out of doors. Would you ladies like to come with me while I inspect my horse Penny? I must be sure she is being well cared for."

Grandfather pretended to look stern, which made the girls laugh out loud. Grandfather knew

that no horse in Virginia was better cared for than
Penny. More than a year ago, Felicity had secretly
befriended Penny and then helped her run away
from Jiggy Nye, the cruel man who claimed to
own her. Felicity and Penny found each other
again in the summer, while Felicity was visiting
Grandfather's plantation. Grandfather bought
Penny and allowed Felicity to bring her beloved
horse back to Williamsburg with her.

"I think you will be pleased with Penny," said
Felicity. She led Grandfather and Elizabeth into
the stable behind the Merrimans' house. It smelled
of horses, leather, and straw. "She's not skittish
anymore, and she's stout and healthy." Felicity
handed her doll to Elizabeth. Then she backed
Penny out of her stall. Penny stood calmly while
Grandfather patted her neck and stroked her sides.

"Stout, indeed!" said Grandfather in a pleased
voice. "Penny is going to have a foal
this spring."

"Oh!" gasped Felicity and
Elizabeth together.

"How wonderful!" said Felicity.
"When will the foal be born?"

foal

"Stout, indeed!" said Grandfather.
"Penny is going to have a foal this spring."

"I can't be certain," said Grandfather. "But I think Penny will be ready to foal in two or three months."

Felicity stroked Penny's neck and asked, "Will she be all right, Grandfather? Will it harm her to have a foal?"

"Penny is young and strong," said Grandfather. "She should come through the birthing well, as long as there are no unusual problems."

"Oh, Grandfather," said Felicity. "I hope you'll be here in Williamsburg when the foal is born. I won't know what to do when it happens."

"I shall try to be here," said Grandfather. "But your father and Marcus know very well how to help Penny. Indeed, they've known for a long while that Penny is with foal. They wanted me to have the pleasure of telling you." He coughed and cleared his throat. "It is too cold in this stable for my old bones. Shall we go inside now and tell your mother the news about Penny?"

"Aye," said Felicity. She led Penny into her stall and gave her one last hug. Then she followed Grandfather and Elizabeth to the house, smiling to herself. *Penny is going to have a foal!* she thought.

What a wonderful spring this will be!

Mother, Nan, and William were sitting by the fire in the parlor. Mother held baby Polly in her arms. Polly was a month old. She was a plump, rosy baby with sky-blue eyes and hair as orange as carrots. Nan held the fire screen to protect Polly's face from the heat of the fire, and William was making a jumping jack dance to amuse her.

fire screen

The baby waved her tiny arms and gurgled.

"Mother!" exclaimed Felicity. "Penny is going to have a foal in the spring! Grandfather just told us! Isn't it wonderful?"

"Aye!" agreed Mrs. Merriman. "It's very fine indeed!"

"A foal!" said Nan. "Oh, Lissie, how lovely!"

"May I ride it?" asked William. "May I ride the foal?"

"You'll have to wait for the foal to grow a bit first, William," said Mother. "Perhaps you can help Felicity care for it."

"Aye," said Grandfather "Felicity will have to give it a lot of good care."

7

"Felicity has been a wonderful help taking care of her baby sister," said Mother. "I'm sure she'll do a fine job with Penny's foal, too."

"Oh, I love taking care of Polly!" said Felicity. "And I'll love caring for Penny's foal. I can't wait till it's born! It's such a happy thing to look forward to."

Grandfather took baby Polly from Mother's arms. "Nothing is happier than a new life starting," he said. He kissed the baby's round cheek. "Nothing is sweeter than a baby. Isn't that right, Polly?"

Polly cooed and Mother smiled.

"Mother," said Felicity, "may Elizabeth and I go to the store and tell Ben? He'll be so pleased to hear about Penny's foal."

"You may go," said Mrs. Merriman, "but remember to put on your pattens. The streets are dreadfully muddy from all the rain we've had."

pattens

"Yes, Mother," said Felicity. She tickled Polly under her soft chin, and then she and Elizabeth left.

Felicity's pattens lifted her feet above the mud, but it was hard to run or skip while wearing them. So Felicity and Elizabeth walked as quickly as they could to Mr. Merriman's store. The streets of Williamsburg were crowded these days. Men from all over the colony were coming to Williamsburg to join the army that was forming to fight against the king's soldiers.

Mr. Merriman's store was full of customers. Many of the men wore dark, fringed hunting shirts that were the uniform of Virginia soldiers. The store smelled of spices and soap and wood smoke. Felicity grinned. She loved her father's store, especially when it was full of people and noise and activity, as it was today. Sometimes lately, when the store was very busy, Mr. Merriman let Felicity work there. She always felt proud and very grown-up when she stood behind the counter. *Maybe I can help out today*, she thought.

Elizabeth tugged at her sleeve and pointed toward the back of the store. "There's Ben," she said. "He's helping that tall man."

Both girls waved. Ben nodded to them and came over as soon as he was free. "How may I help you ladies today?" he asked.

"Ben!" exclaimed Felicity. "We have the most wonderful news! Penny is going to have a foal this spring!"

"A foal!" said Ben. He smiled. "Good for Penny! Her foal will be the finest in all of Virginia, I'm sure!"

Mr. Merriman joined them with a laugh. "So your grandfather told you the news about Penny!" he said. "I knew you'd be happy, Lissie. No one loves horses more than you do." He turned to Ben and said, "That reminds me, Ben. Have you delivered the currycombs Mr. Pelham ordered for his horses?"

"No, sir," said Ben. "Not yet."

"I know you have been busy," said Mr. Merriman, "but 'tis bad to make Mr. Pelham wait."

"We'll do it!" Felicity offered. "Elizabeth and I can make the delivery for you, Father."

"Very well," said Mr. Merriman. "I might have known that you would volunteer when you heard there were horses involved!" He handed Felicity a bundle wrapped in paper. "Mr. Pelham will pay you. Bring the money back to me." Just then, someone called for Mr. Merriman. "Ben and I had better go back to work," he said. "Thank you for your help, girls!"

CHAPTER
TWO

—

FRIENDS DIVIDED

Felicity and Elizabeth set forth to deliver the currycombs to Mr. Pelham, the town jailer. He lived in a little house next to the jail, which stood at the edge of Williamsburg.

"Lissie," said Elizabeth, as they walked, "is Mr. Nye still in jail?"

"Yes," said Felicity, "and I am very glad he is. As long as he is in jail, I don't have to worry that he'll come bother Penny."

"He won't be in jail forever," said Elizabeth. "Someday he'll pay the debt he owes and get out of jail."

"I suppose so," said Felicity. She stepped around a puddle.

"Well," Elizabeth asked, "when he does get out of jail, what will you do?"

Felicity shuddered. "Nothing at all," she said firmly. "I don't want to have *anything* to do with Mr. Nye. He's mean."

"Maybe you could speak to him," said Elizabeth. "Maybe you could make him promise to stay away from Penny and her foal. Maybe—"

"Humph!" snorted Felicity. "You don't know him, Elizabeth. A promise from Mr. Nye isn't worth dust."

Elizabeth said no more. They had reached Mr. Pelham's house. It was connected to the jail, which looked gloomy even in the afternoon sunshine. Felicity knocked on Mr. Pelham's stout wooden door. She and Elizabeth waited on the doorstep for a few minutes. At last, Mr. Pelham opened the door.

"Yes?" he said. "What is it?"

"Good afternoon, sir," said Felicity. "We're delivering your currycombs from Merriman's store." She held out the bundle.

"Ah, yes, indeed," said Mr. Pelham. "Thank you! 'Tis good of you to bring them to my house! Come in for a moment while I find money to pay you."

The two girls stepped inside Mr. Pelham's house as he went on, "I don't have time to get to the store these days. The jail is crowded since they've started arresting Loyalists. I'm so busy, I just . . ." He stopped and looked around. "Oh bother!" he said. "I've left my money in my coat pocket, and I've left my coat in the passage. If you'll just follow me . . ."

He lit a candle and led the girls to the passage that connected his house to the jail. "Come along this way," he said. "I've got the—"

Suddenly, they all heard a muffled thump, and then someone started coughing violently and choking. Felicity realized she was standing next to the door of a cell. The sounds came from inside.

"Oh dear!" exclaimed Mr. Pelham. "Stay right here, girls! I've got to help." His keys jangled as he hurriedly unlocked the door and rushed into the cell.

Felicity and Elizabeth shivered a little. But they couldn't help peering after him. The cell was small and cold and dark. Mr. Pelham had set his candle on the floor. By its eerie light, the girls saw the jailer easing a man's body back onto a pallet. The body sagged as if it had no bones. The head rolled toward them and Felicity gasped.

The man's eyes were closed. His skin was ghostly white. He was shrunken and thin enough to seem almost transparent. But Felicity was sure that the lifeless lump on the pallet was her old enemy. She swallowed hard and whispered to Elizabeth, "That is Mr. Nye!"

Elizabeth's eyes widened, but she said nothing. Both girls stepped back quickly as Mr. Pelham came out of the cell and locked the door behind him.

"That's Mr. Nye, isn't it?" Felicity asked.

"Aye," said Mr. Pelham.

"Is he . . . is he dead?" Elizabeth whispered.

"Near to it," said Mr. Pelham. "He's had the fever for days. He's got no money to buy logs for a fire, or a blanket, or medicine." The jailer shook his head. "Jiggy Nye used to be a respected man. No one in Williamsburg knew more about animals. But after his wife died, he took to drinking. He drank in hate with every drop. He's been in the stocks and pillory many times. Now he's ended up here, in debtors' jail,

stocks   pillory

Felicity swallowed hard and whispered to Elizabeth,
"That is Mr. Nye!"

with no one to care if he lives or dies."

After Mr. Pelham paid for the currycombs, Felicity and Elizabeth said good-bye. The sky was a wintry pink as they walked away from the jail. Felicity felt cold. She pulled her cloak close around her. But the chill she felt was inside and would not go away.

Felicity and Elizabeth walked together silently through the January dusk. Mr. Nye's face haunted Felicity. She could not forget how helpless and sad he looked. Then Felicity shook herself. *Mr. Nye might be sick,* she thought, *but he is still the man who treated Penny so badly. I will not feel sorry for him. . . .*

Elizabeth looked over at Felicity. "It was terrible in that cell, wasn't it?" she said. "It was so dark and so cold. No one should have to live in a place like that, especially someone who is sick, with no one to care for him."

Felicity said firmly, "It is Mr. Nye's own fault he has no friends. He is cold-hearted and cruel."

"He looked like a weak, helpless old man to me," said Elizabeth softly.

"Maybe so, but you don't know him!" said Felicity.

"That is true," said Elizabeth. She faced Felicity. "Don't you feel sorry for him at all?" she asked.

"Well," said Felicity. "He did look miserable. But after the way he treated Penny, I could never feel sorry for him."

"I think we should bring him a blanket and some medicine," said Elizabeth. She sounded gentle but determined. "I think we should help him."

"No!" said Felicity. "Not Mr. Nye! He would never accept anything from me anyway. He hates me as much as I hate him."

"He doesn't need to know it's from you," said Elizabeth. "No one needs to know."

"Elizabeth," said Felicity, "even if I did feel sorry for him, a little bit, why should I be kind to him? Why should I help him? If he does get better, he may come looking for Penny."

"Then that's when you tell him you were the one who helped him," said Elizabeth. "He won't hate you if you've been kind to him. He won't hurt Penny."

"It won't do any good," said Felicity. "Mr. Nye will never change."

"Aye, you are right," said Elizabeth. "He won't

18

change if you do nothing. But if you help him, there is a chance he *will* change."

"You don't understand," said Felicity. "Mr. Nye said he would kill Penny before he'd let me have her. He meant it, too."

"He may have meant it when he said it," replied Elizabeth. "But if you do something nice for him, he won't want to hurt you or your horse. Don't you see, Felicity? If you help him, you will be doing something to protect Penny and her foal."

Felicity thought about what Elizabeth had said. After a long while she turned and said, "Very well. I'll do it. But only because of Penny."

"Good!" said Elizabeth.

"I have an old horse blanket we can give him," said Felicity, "and Mother and I made garlic syrup for Grandfather's cold. I'll mix up more."

"I can bring a blanket, too," said Elizabeth. "I'll come to your house tomorrow at three o'clock. Then we'll go to the jail."

"Tomorrow at three," repeated Felicity as the girls parted to go to their homes.

But Elizabeth did not come to Felicity's house the next day at three o'clock. Felicity was puzzled. She waited almost an hour, and then she went to Elizabeth's house to find her.

Felicity was carrying a basket with a bottle of medicine and the old horse blanket in it. She had pinned a note to the blanket that said, *For Mr. Nye*. The basket was heavy. It banged against Felicity's knees with every step.

Felicity knocked on the door of the Coles' house for a long time before a servant answered. He opened the door just a bit and stuck his head out. "I'm very sorry, miss," he said. He sounded flustered. "Mrs. Cole and her daughters are not receiving callers." He started to close the door.

"Wait!" Felicity exclaimed. "You know me. I'm Felicity Merriman, Elizabeth's friend. Whatever is the matter? Why can't I see Elizabeth?"

"I beg your pardon, Miss Felicity," the servant said. "You can't come in. I'm sorry. You'll have to go." He closed the door quite firmly.

Felicity was confused and worried. *Something awful must have happened!* she thought. *Someone must*

be terribly sick. I wonder if it's Elizabeth! Felicity
didn't know what to do. She knocked on the door
again, but no one came. She looked up at the
window of Elizabeth's room, but she couldn't see
anything. She walked around to the back of the
house. Everything was shut tight, as if the Coles
had gone away.

Felicity gave up. She walked to the jail without
thinking about where she was going. She had just
put the basket next to the doorstep of Mr. Pelham's
house when the door opened. Quickly, she stood in
front of the basket to hide it.

"Oh, it's you again," said Mr. Pelham. "Why
are you back?"

"I . . . I think I left something here," said Felicity.

"Well, I haven't time to help look for it," said
Mr. Pelham impatiently. "I'm busy. They've just
brought another Loyalist here. I don't know how
I'm supposed to find room for him. The jail's
overcrowded as it is without this new one, this fine
and fancy gentleman, Mr. Cole."

Mr. Cole? Elizabeth's father? Felicity was
stunned. "It can't be Mr. Cole," she said to the
jailer. "Why would Mr. Cole be put in jail?"

21

"He's a Loyalist," shrugged Mr. Pelham. "That's reason enough."

"But that's not fair!" Felicity exclaimed. "Mr. Cole hasn't done anything wrong! You can't—"

"Now, miss!" interrupted Mr. Pelham. "I didn't arrest him! And I can't stand here arguing with you. You'll have to go." He closed the door.

Felicity turned away. She could not believe what she'd heard. Elizabeth's father was in jail! He was locked away in a cold, dark cell just like a horse thief. And all because he was a Loyalist. *No wonder I wasn't allowed into the Coles' house today,* she thought. *They know Father is a Patriot. They probably don't trust anyone in the colony today.*

Felicity knew there had been battles between the king's soldiers and the Patriots' army in Massachusetts and Canada and nearby Norfolk. She had seen soldiers with their guns, training to fight, right on Market Square in Williamsburg. But none of that had affected anyone she loved. Now it seemed that what she had feared most was happening. The fight between the Patriots and the Loyalists was

the king's soldiers

changing everything. It was going to separate her from her friend.

Suddenly Felicity wanted to see her own father. She wanted to be sure he was safe, and to feel safe herself. She ran to Father's store.

Father, Grandfather, and Ben were talking in Father's office. It was warm there, and gently lit by candles. Father smiled as Felicity came in. "Your grandfather and I can't agree about when Penny's foal is going to be born," he said. "I think it will be sooner than . . . " He stopped when he saw Felicity's face in the light. "Why, Lissie!" he said. "What's the matter?"

"Patriots put Mr. Cole in jail," said Felicity, "just because he is a Loyalist."

"Elizabeth's father?" gasped Ben. "In jail?"

"Aye!" said Felicity. "In a cold, dark cell, just like Mr. Nye!"

"This is an outrage!" exclaimed Grandfather. He was furious. "This just cannot be possible!"

"I'm afraid anything is possible these days," said Mr. Merriman.

"The Coles' servant wouldn't even allow me to talk to Elizabeth," said Felicity. "Does Mrs.

Cole think I'm an enemy because you're a Patriot, Father?"

Father put his arm around Felicity's shoulder. "Elizabeth knows you are her friend," he said. "Never fear."

Ben tried to comfort her, too. "The day after next is Sunday," he said. "You'll see Elizabeth at church. You'll be able to speak to her there."

Felicity hoped he was right.

CHAPTER
THREE

—

GRANDFATHER'S
ERRAND

Sunday morning was gray and bitterly cold. Felicity kept her hands in her mitts and muff as the family walked to church. She held tightly to something special she'd tucked inside her muff to give Elizabeth if she had the chance. She looked for Elizabeth in the churchyard but did not see her.

The service had just begun when a whisper swept through the church. Felicity looked around to see Mrs. Cole leading Elizabeth and her sister Annabelle down the aisle. Mrs. Cole held her head high. Elizabeth's face was hidden by the hood of her blue cloak. Felicity could not catch her eye.

After the service, the Coles left the church

quickly. Felicity hurried after them. "Elizabeth!" she
called. "Wait!"

Elizabeth turned around, but Mrs. Cole took
her firmly by the hand and pulled her away.
Felicity ran to catch up. "Elizabeth!" she said. "Take
this!" From her muff she pulled the sampler of
stitches she had finished last spring. There was a
bluebird on it, just the color of Elizabeth's cloak.
And under the bluebird it said: *Faithful Friends
Forever Be.* Felicity thrust the sampler into
Elizabeth's hand.

Elizabeth looked at it and gave Felicity a sad

smile before her mother hurried her away.

Felicity felt Grandfather's hand on her shoulder. Together, they watched Elizabeth disappear. "I hate to see Elizabeth so unhappy," said Felicity. "I wish I could break open the jail! I wish I could smash the door down and help Mr. Cole escape! I want to do something, *anything*, to help."

"I'm sure you do," said Grandfather. "I do, too."

Icy rain fell all that day, all night long, and on into the morning. The next day the ground was slick and the trees groaned under a coating of ice. Mrs. Merriman would not allow the children to go out of doors. They played together in front of the parlor fire. Felicity sat on the floor with baby Polly in her lap. It was comforting to hold Polly's warm little body, and spin the top for her, and listen to her coo with delight.

"Felicity," asked Mother, "have you seen Grandfather this morning?"

"No, Mother," said Felicity. "Not since breakfast."

"Oh, dear," fretted Mrs. Merriman. "He's gone out in this weather! It will make his cold worse!"

She looked out the window at the freezing rain. "Why didn't he wait until the rain stopped? What urgent errand could he have had?"

Felicity could see that her mother was very worried. "I don't know, Mother," she said. "Grandfather didn't say anything to me."

Mrs. Merriman grew more and more worried as she waited for Grandfather to return. It was almost dinnertime before they heard him come in the door. Mrs. Merriman ran to greet him. "Where have you been?" she fussed. "You're soaked to the skin! I'll take your cloak. Go and sit by the fire."

Grandfather sank into the chair by the fire. His face was pale. He sounded tired when he said, "Felicity, come here."

Felicity put Polly in her cradle and went over to stand next to Grandfather's chair. "Yes, Grandfather?" she said.

Grandfather coughed and cleared his throat. "My business today had to do with you," he said, "and your friend Elizabeth and her family. I went to see her father today."

"You went to the jail?" asked Felicity.

"Yes," said Grandfather. He shivered. "What a

dismal, dreadful place it is! I spoke to Mr. Cole. He is a fine gentleman. After our conversation, I went to the authorities."

Mother gasped. Grandfather went on to say, "Now that the king's royal governor is gone, Williamsburg is governed by the Committee of Safety. The chairman of the committee is Edmund Pendleton."

Grandfather paused for breath. His eyes had a bit of their old twinkle in them. "Well!" he said. "I've known Pendleton since he was a young pup! I went straight to him, and I said, 'Stop this nonsense, Pendleton! Release Mr. Cole. I have his word as a gentleman that he has not caused any trouble. And if you need another Loyalist to fill Mr. Cole's place in jail, take me!'"

Grandfather laughed so hard he made himself cough. When he could speak again, he said, "I wish you could have seen Pendleton's face. It was as purple as a turnip! He mumbled and chattered about how being a Loyalist was treasonous to Virginia. He said he would have to present the matter to the Committee of Safety and then speak to Mr. Cole himself. He blustered and fussed, but in the end he had to admit that Mr. Cole had done nothing wrong, so he would try to have him released."

"Does that mean Mr. Cole will go home?" asked William.

"Yes," said Grandfather. "I believe he will go home."

"Hurray!" shouted Nan and William.

"Oh, Grandfather!" exclaimed Felicity. "Thank you! Elizabeth will be so happy!" She kissed his cheek. "I'm happy, too."

Mother's eyes were full of love as she looked at Grandfather. "It's a fine thing you've done this morning," she said. "I hope it hasn't been too much for you."

"I do feel a bit feverish," admitted Grandfather. "I'd like to rest now. Don't worry about my dinner. I'm more tired than hungry."

Felicity helped him out of his chair. He leaned on her as he went slowly up the stairs to his chamber. He seemed worn-out and frail. But as Felicity was closing his door behind her, she heard him chuckle and say to himself, "Pendleton, hah! Purple as a turnip he was!" She smiled and skipped down the stairs. Grandfather had set everything right.

❧

After dinner, Felicity asked her mother, "May I go see Elizabeth now?"

"No, I don't think you should," said Mother. "This has been very hard on Mrs. Cole. It may take some time for her to feel friendly toward any family that supports the Patriots. We must wait and see how she feels about your friendship with Elizabeth. You had better wait for Mrs. Cole to allow Elizabeth to come to you. Be patient."

Felicity was disappointed. She was aching to see her friend. She decided to go to Father's store. Its cheery bustle always made her happy, and she wanted to tell Father what Grandfather had done for Mr. Cole.

Felicity took the long way around to the store so that she could walk past Elizabeth's house. She stopped in front. Sleet stung her eyes as she looked up at Elizabeth's window. She couldn't see any movement inside, just something propped on the

windowsill. Felicity squinted to see better. It was a
needlework frame holding the sampler Felicity had
given to Elizabeth. Felicity wanted to
dance for happiness. She knew
Elizabeth meant the message for her:
Faithful Friends Forever Be.

The next day, a pale winter sun shone, but it
wasn't warm enough to melt the brittle ice coating
the trees. Felicity was up early. As she led Penny
from her stall to exercise her, Ben came down from
his room above the stable.

"Good morning!" he said. "How is Penny
today?"

"She's fine," said Felicity. "Father says I
shouldn't ride her. He thinks her foal will be born
quite soon."

Ben followed along as Felicity walked Penny
around the stable yard.

"Well," he said with a grin. "I don't know
much about foals, but Penny is so big, I'd say your
Father is right."

"I'm glad you'll be here when it's born," said

Felicity. "If you had run away to be a soldier in General Washington's army, you'd never have known about Penny's foal."

Ben looked serious. "I promised your father I'd stay at the store until I'm eighteen," he said. "I won't break my promise. But when that day comes, I'll go fight with the Patriots. I won't change my mind about that. Not ever."

Felicity sighed. "You're just as stubborn as Grandfather," she said. "He'll never change his mind about the king. He'll always be a Loyalist."

"Your Grandfather and I will never agree," Ben said. He and Felicity led Penny back to the stable and into her stall. "But I do respect him."

"I do, too!" agreed Felicity. "I'm so happy that he helped Mr. Cole. Grandfather made everything all right again, just as it was before."

"No, Lissie," said Ben sadly. "Not even your grandfather could do that."

But Felicity ran ahead of Ben to the house, so she did not hear him.

"Where's Grandfather?" she asked, as she sat at the breakfast table.

"The fever is much worse," said Mother, "and

'tis hard for him to breathe. Rose has mixed some molasses, vinegar, and butter for him to drink to ease the pain in his throat. Father and Mr. Galt, the apothecary, are with him now."

Ben, Felicity, Nan, and William looked at each other. They knew by the way Mother spoke that Grandfather was very ill. After breakfast, Ben left for the store. The children went into the parlor. They played quietly with Polly.

Soon after Father and the apothecary left, Mother came into the parlor. Felicity could tell she had been crying. "Felicity," Mother said, "Grand-father is asking for you."

Felicity hurried up the stairs and tiptoed into Grandfather's shadowy chamber. Grandfather was lying very still. His breathing was slow and his skin was ashy gray. Felicity stood next to him and took his hand. Grandfather opened his eyes.

"Don't try to talk, Grandfather," said Felicity softly. "You just lie there. I'll read to you."

Grandfather closed his eyes again.

Felicity read from the Bible. "The Lord is my shepherd," she read, "therefore I lack nothing. He shall feed me in a green pasture; and lead me forth

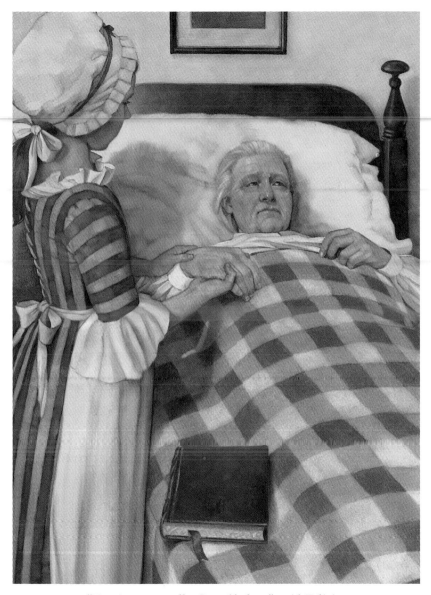

"Don't try to talk, Grandfather," said Felicity.
"You just lie there. I'll read to you."

beside the waters of comfort. . . . "

Felicity looked at Grandfather. "That part always makes me think of your plantation," she said. "I imagine lying in the green grass in the big pasture on the hill on a sunny day. And the river is comforting. It's peaceful, the way it flows along so smoothly. You'll be back there soon, Grandfather. You'll feel fine once you get back to your plantation."

Grandfather reached up and stroked her cheek. "Dear Lissie," he whispered. He sighed and went to sleep. Felicity kissed his forehead and then tiptoed away.

Days passed, and Grandfather grew weaker and weaker. One night, after Felicity and Nan went to bed in the chamber they were sharing while Grandfather visited, Felicity heard voices and saw light moving in the passage outside their door. She thought the apothecary had probably come back again. Nan woke up, too. They lay in the dark, listening.

In a little while, the door opened and Mother came in. She put the candlestick on the table, sat on the bed, and took each of them by the hand.

"My dear girls," she said in a shaky voice. "Your grandfather died . . . just a few minutes ago." Her voice faltered, and then she said softly, "He loved you both very, very much. God rest his soul."

Nan cried bitterly. Felicity was silent as she clung to her mother. Her sorrow was too great to be eased by crying. Mother sat with Nan and Felicity until the sky lightened to gray and the last star disappeared.

INTO THE VALLEY

Grandfather's burial was to take place at his plantation on the York River, a few hours' ride from Williamsburg. Mother and the children rode together in a carriage. Father rode on horseback. Marcus drove the cart that carried Grandfather's coffin. The roads were muddy and so deeply rutted that the carriage jolted and swayed. Felicity hardly noticed. She felt numb, as if all the life in her had died, too.

As they rode up the drive to Grandfather's plantation, Felicity looked out at the dreary landscape. When she had last seen the plantation, at the end of the summer, it was alive with color. Now the pastures were brown, the trees inky black, and the river a cold, dull silver. Her first view of the river used to make Felicity's spirits soar. Today she felt no joy.

Grandfather was buried on a windy bluff above the river. Felicity set her jaw and would not allow herself to cry as she listened to the minister read the end of the psalm she had read to Grandfather. "Yea, though I walk through the valley of the shadow of death, I will fear no evil . . ."

The words did not comfort her. Felicity was angry at the world and angry at the God who had taken her grandfather away from her. She was fearful, too. Nothing seemed safe anymore. How could she trust a world where such sorrowful things as death happened? How could she feel safe when Grandfather was not there to protect her, understand her, and love her? She was glad the blustery wind blew the minister's words away.

After supper, the children were sent to bed. Felicity wasn't sleepy. She sat by the window watching the gray sky turn black.

"Felicity," she heard Mother say. She turned. Mother stood behind her, holding a small trunk. "This was

in Grandfather's chamber. He meant to give it
to you on your birthday. I think you should have
it now."

She put the trunk on the floor, and Felicity
knelt to open it. She lifted out a riding habit made
of deep green wool, the color of forest pines. At
the sight of it, all the tears Felicity had been
holding back burst forth. *Oh, Grandfather*, Felicity
thought. *You and I will never ride together again. I
will never be able to thank you for this, or laugh with
you, or hug you ever again.* Felicity buried her face
in her arms and sobbed.

Mother knelt beside her and put her arms
around Felicity. "It makes me so sad," gasped
Felicity, "when I think of riding with Grandfather . . ."

"Aye," said Mother. "Memories can make your
heart ache with sorrow. But it is good to remember
happy times with your Grandfather. Indeed, as
long as you remember him, he won't be truly gone
from you."

"But he *is* gone," said Felicity passionately.
"Oh, I wish I could go back. I want to go back to
this summer, when Grandfather was well and we

"I want to go back to this summer, when Grandfather was well and we were all so happy together!"

were all so happy together!"

"I understand," said Mother. She looked out the window. "This plantation is where I grew up," she said. "Sometimes when I am here, I ask myself, would I go back and be a child, be with my mother and father again, if I could? Those were lovely days." She paused, and then said, "But then I think . . . ah, how could I live without my sweet Lissie, and Nan, and William, and Polly? How could I be happy without my dear husband? No, as much as I miss my mother and now my father, I wouldn't go back, even if I could. That's as it should be. We're meant to grow and learn and change."

"No!" said Felicity. "I hate changes!"

"Not all changes are bad," said Mrs. Merriman. "Think of how you've changed in the past year. You're not the flighty, headstrong child you used to be. You're steady and thoughtful, even if you are still sometimes impatient. And think of all the happy changes you have to look forward to. You'll see Elizabeth again. You'll see Polly learn to walk and talk and become a little person. You'll see Penny's foal be born and grow up." She brushed the tears from Felicity's cheek. "Face those changes with faith and hope, my child, not fear."

"How can I hope for anything, when Grandfather is dead?" asked Felicity. "Death is the end of everything."

"No," said Mother. "No change, no loss, no separation, not even death, can end love." She kissed Felicity's flushed forehead and left.

Felicity cried until she felt hollow. After a long while, she fell asleep.

Mother and the children went home a few days after Grandfather's burial. As the carriage lurched along the road to Williamsburg, William asked, "Mother, why isn't Father coming home, too?"

"Your father and Marcus stayed at the plantation to put Grandfather's business affairs in order," said Mother. "They'll be home soon."

William looked as if he might cry. "But I don't want Father gone," he said. "I want him to be home with us."

Felicity felt sorry for William. *He's probably afraid Father will go away forever, like Grandfather*, she thought. "Don't worry, William," she said. "Father will be home before you know it. And meanwhile, Mother and I will look after you, and you and Nan must help us look after baby Polly."

William brightened, and Mother smiled at Felicity gratefully.

Ben was at the front door of the house to greet them as the carriage pulled up. He helped Mrs. Merriman step down. "Thank you, Ben," she said. "Mr. Merriman and Marcus will be gone for a few weeks. Will you be able to take care of the store in their absence?"

"Yes, ma'am," said Ben.

"Good lad," said Mrs. Merriman. She turned to Felicity. "I am sure Ben could use an extra pair of hands today, Lissie," she said. "Would you like to help him in the store?"

"Yes," said Felicity. "Yes, I would."

"Off you go then," said Mother. She knew that no place was more likely to cheer Felicity than her father's store.

And indeed, the store was so bustling all

afternoon, Felicity was too busy
to be sad. She and Ben walked
home together in the twilight
after they closed the store.
"Thank you for your help," said
Ben. "You know just what to do
in the store. You were a good apprentice today."

Felicity just nodded.

Ben looked at her. "Lissie," he said, "I know
you are very sad about your grandfather. I'm
sorry, too. He was a fine old gentleman. No one
can replace him." They walked on, and then Ben
said, "You helped me when I was hurt and . . .
and unhappy this summer. I wish I could help
you now."

Felicity smiled for the first time in a long
time. "Thank you, Ben," she said. "You are a
kind friend."

❧

Over the next few days, the air seemed to soften.
It sometimes carried hints that spring was coming.
Sorrow still overcame Felicity whenever she thought
about Grandfather. There were reminders of him

everywhere. Whenever she heard music, or when she played the guitar he had given her, Felicity thought of her grandfather's gravelly voice singing along, happily out of tune. Whenever she cared for Penny, she remembered the day Grandfather had told her she could bring Penny back to Williamsburg with her. Whenever she held Polly, she thought of how Grandfather had said, *Nothing is happier than a new life starting. Nothing is sweeter than a baby.*

She was thinking of Grandfather one afternoon as she worked in her garden, pulling away dead leaves to prepare the ground for spring planting, just as he had taught her. Felicity looked up and saw Elizabeth running toward her, her familiar blue cloak flying behind her as she ran.

"Felicity!" gasped Elizabeth, all out of breath. "Oh, I am so glad to see you!"

Felicity hugged her friend. "I am glad to see you, too!" she said.

Elizabeth's eyes filled with tears. "When I heard that your grandfather died, my heart ached for you," she said. "And Mother felt so sorry. She never thanked him for getting Father released from jail."

"You must be happy to have your father home

now," said Felicity.

"Aye," said Elizabeth. "He will be home for a while. But he had to promise to leave the colony. He's going to New York. It's safer for Loyalists there."

"New York!" exclaimed Felicity. "Oh, no! Oh, Elizabeth! You are not going to leave, too, are you?"

"No," said Elizabeth. "Mother and Annabelle and I will stay here to look after our property."

"Ah," said Felicity. "You will miss your father most terribly, won't you?"

"I will," said Elizabeth. "But at least I know

he'll be safe, and not in that awful jail." She sighed. "Mother and Annabelle and I will have to take care of ourselves. Things are different now. Many things have changed."

"Aye," said Felicity sadly. "Everything has changed."

"I know one thing that has not changed," said Elizabeth. "You are still my best friend."

The girls smiled at each other.

"I thought about you every day," said Elizabeth. "I wondered what you were doing. Did you ever go to the jail?"

"Yes," said Felicity. "I left a blanket and some medicine by the door."

"I wonder if Mr. Nye got them," said Elizabeth. "I wonder if he's better now, or if he . . ."

Felicity had been wondering the very same things. "Perhaps we could go to the jail," she said. "Perhaps we could ask Mr. Pelham about Mr. Nye."

"Yes!" said Elizabeth. "Let's go now!"

Mr. Pelham's smile was wide when he saw the girls at the door of his house. "Good day, young ladies!" he said. "What are you delivering today?"

"Mr. Pelham," said Felicity, "we came to ask about someone. We were wondering . . . how is Mr. Nye?"

"He's not here!" said Mr. Pelham happily. "He paid his debt. He's gone."

"But he was so ill," said Felicity, "and he had no money, or friends . . . "

"Bless my soul!" said Mr. Pelham. "It turned out that Jiggy Nye *did* have friends. Soon after you two young ladies came to deliver the currycombs, the most curious thing happened. I found a basket outside this very door with a blanket and some medicine in it for Jiggy Nye. I never did see who left it." He looked at Felicity and Elizabeth. "Was it the two of you together?"

"No," said Elizabeth in her sweet voice. "It was not the two of us together."

Mr. Pelham went on, "Well, then the most curious thing of all happened a few days later! Along came an old gentleman. His health was poor but his spirit was strong. He came to the jail to see that other gentleman, the Loyalist, Mr. Cole. After he spoke to Mr. Cole, he asked to see Jiggy Nye."

Felicity and Elizabeth looked at each other in amazement. They knew Mr. Pelham was talking about Grandfather.

"I told the old gentleman that Mr. Nye was too ill to talk," said Mr. Pelham. "He left me money and told me to tell Jiggy Nye that he owed him the money for a horse. He said something about a penny, but he left me a great deal more money than that! When Mr. Nye was better, I gave him the money. He understood the old gentleman's message even if I didn't. Mr. Nye used the money to pay off most of his debt. He's working for me, caring for my horses, to pay off the rest of it. He's a good man with animals when he's not drinking. And I think from now on he'll stay away from the bottle."

Mr. Pelham smiled again. "That blanket and medicine did more than help cure Jiggy Nye of his illness. It seemed to cure him of his meanness, too. I always thought there was still some goodness left in old Jiggy Nye. And I was right. It just needed the kindness of friends to bring it out."

Felicity's heart was too full for her to speak.

Grandfather had given Mr. Nye money for Penny. Grandfather *had* fixed everything. Thanks to his kindness, she needn't fear Mr. Nye or what he might do to Penny or her foal. *Thank you, Grandfather,* she thought. *Oh, thank you!*

CHAPTER
FIVE
—

PATRIOT

"Felicity! Wake up!"

Felicity woke from a deep sleep to see Mother and Ben standing next to her bed. "What is it?" she asked. "What's the matter?"

"It's Penny," said Ben. "I think she's going to have her foal."

"Oh, no!" said Felicity. She jumped out of bed and pulled on stockings and shoes as Mother wrapped a cloak around her. "Father is gone and so is Marcus! What shall we do?"

"There's no need to fret," said Mother, as they all hurried out to the stable. "Penny will be fine."

Ben lit a lantern and hung it on a nail in Penny's stall. Penny was lying on the straw. Her sides were heaving.

Felicity knelt down and stroked Penny's neck. "Penny! Penny, my girl," murmured Felicity. "Oh, Penny! Are you all right?"

Ben looked worried. "The foal is having trouble," he said. "Something is not right. I don't know what to do. We need to get help."

Felicity stood up. "Mother, you hold Penny's head and try to keep her quiet," she said. "I'll go get help."

"Take the lantern!" called Mother.

But Felicity did not need the lantern, though the night was starless. She knew the way through the garden, through the dark streets, past the sleeping houses, to the edge of town. She had run this way many, many times on those cool mornings before dawn when she had sneaked off to see Penny in the pasture. She knew exactly where she was going to find Mr. Nye.

Mr. Nye's house was a tumble-down shack next to the tannery. It looked ghostly and forbidding, blacker than the night around it. Felicity pounded on the door. "Mr. Nye! Mr. Nye!" she cried. "Please! Please help me!"

The door opened and Mr. Nye stood there, holding a candle that cast light on his craggy face. "You!" he said, when he saw Felicity.

"You've got to help us, Mr. Nye," said Felicity. "Penny's having her foal. Something's wrong. Mr. Pelham, the jailer, said you know all about animals. Please, will you come help?"

Mr. Nye stared at Felicity. "It was you, wasn't it, who brought that blanket and the medicine to me?" he said in his gruff voice. "And it was your grandfather who left money for me. Don't say it wasn't. I know it was. I owe you a kindness. I'll come with you now."

"Please, make haste!" said Felicity. "We've no time to spare."

Never in her wildest dreams could Felicity have imagined she would be running through the night with Mr. Nye, very glad that he was by her side. But she was. Together, they ran to the Merrimans' stable and hurried inside. When Mr. Nye came into the lantern light and Mother and Ben saw him, they looked horrified.

"What are *you* doing here?" Ben said. "Get away! If you hurt Felicity or Penny, I'll kill you.

54

"You've got to help us, Mr. Nye," said Felicity.

Mark me, I will!"

"It's all right, Ben," explained Felicity. "I brought him here. He knows how to help Penny."

Ben looked confused. "It's all right, Ben," Felicity said again. "He is a friend."

Mr. Nye turned to Felicity. "You'll have to keep your horse calm," he said. "If she moves suddenly when she sees me, it'll hurt her and the foal. And I don't reckon she's forgotten or forgiven me for the way I treated her."

"I'll keep her calm," said Felicity. She and her mother knelt by Penny's head. They stroked her and murmured soothing words.

Mr. Nye did not make a sound. All his movements were sure. His touch on Penny was gentle. In a short time, the foal was born.

Felicity looked at the beautiful little colt lying on the straw next to Penny. He was black and shiny, with spindly legs. *Grandfather was right*, she thought. *Nothing is happier than a new life starting.* "Oh, Penny," she whispered. "Your colt is perfect." She hugged Penny, and then she hugged Mother. When she looked up to thank Mr. Nye for his help, he was gone.

Ben grinned at the colt. "He's a gawky little thing, isn't he? But he'll grow into those legs," he said. "He'll be a beauty, just like his mother."

"And just as spirited, too," said Mrs. Merriman.

"Aye," said Felicity. "I am sure this colt will be full of independence, just like Penny."

Ben laughed. "And as full of fire as a Patriot soldier."

"That's what we'll call him," said Felicity. "Patriot."

"Patriot," repeated Mother. "That is a fine, proud name."

By the time Father and Marcus came home, Patriot could already trot around the stable yard on his long, thin legs. "That's the most handsome colt I've ever seen," said Father in a pleased voice as he inspected Patriot. "Felicity, you amaze me. There's not another girl in Virginia who could handle the birth of a foal so well."

"Oh, I did nothing, Father!" said Felicity. She swung herself up onto Penny's back. She and Father were going for a ride. It was Penny's first outing since Patriot had been born. "It was Mr. Nye who helped Penny."

"Jiggy Nye?" said Father. "That scoundrel? You went to him for help?"

"Aye," said Felicity. "He is a friend now."

"That is a change," said Father. He was riding Old Bess.

"It was Elizabeth's idea to help him," said Felicity. "He and I wouldn't have become friends if it were not for her and Grandfather."

Mr. Merriman smiled at Felicity. "You and

Elizabeth are fine young ladies," he said. "I am proud of you. Your grandfather would be proud, too."

Mr. Merriman and Felicity rode side by side along the street in the cool spring sunshine. Felicity sat tall on Penny's back. She was wearing the dark green riding habit from Grandfather. Whenever she wore it, she thought of Grandfather, and how much she loved him, and how much she missed him. Her memories still made her sad, but it was a gentle sadness, not sharp and bitter anymore.

"I miss Grandfather every day," Felicity said to her father.

"Aye," said Father. "He loved you very much." He looked at Felicity seriously. "Your grandfather left his plantation to Mother and you children," he said. "He knew how much you loved it."

"Does that mean we will live on the plantation now?" asked Felicity.

"Is that what you would like to do?" asked Father.

Felicity took a deep breath. She thought of how lovely the plantation was in the summer. The green fields stretched from the river to the forest, and the air was sweet with the scents of fruits and flowers. Life there flowed along as smoothly as the river. Then she looked around her at the busy streets of Williamsburg, full of people and color, noise and life. She thought of Father's store, and Ben, and Elizabeth.

"No, Father," she said. "I'd rather stay here in Williamsburg."

Father nodded at Felicity. "I'm glad you want to stay," he said. "I fear there are hard times ahead. This will be a long war."

"Father," said Felicity as they rode along, "doesn't the king's army have a lot more soldiers than the Patriots' army?"

"Aye," said Father. "But the war for independence isn't only between armies. The king's army will have to defeat more than soldiers. They'll have to defeat the people themselves, you and me, and everyone like us. And as long as our hearts and minds are set on independence, as long as we don't give up, no army can defeat us. The war will touch us all. It will be won or lost by us all."

"Will you be a soldier, Father?" asked Felicity.

"No," said Father. "I don't want to fight with a gun. I'm going to help the Patriots in another way.

I'm going to be a commissary agent. Marcus and I will travel and collect supplies for the Patriots' army. I will be gone a great deal of the time. I'm relying on you to help Mother with the house and the other children. She says you are a wonderful help to her. And you will have to help Ben, too, in the store. You will not have much time for playing."

"Oh! I love working in the store, Father," said Felicity. "You know I always have! And perhaps by helping you, I will be helping the Patriots, too."

"You will indeed," said Father.

"There is another way I can help," said Felicity. She leaned down and stroked Penny's neck. Then she said slowly, "I can give you Penny. You can ride her when you collect supplies."

"Lissie," said Father, "I know you love Penny very much. Wouldn't it be hard for you to be separated from her?"

"Aye," said Felicity softly. "But I will be happy knowing that you and Penny are together, looking after each other. I will trust each of you to bring the other back to me safely."

"You are a fine young lady indeed, Lissie!" said Father. They had reached the pastures at the edge of town. "Come along now! Let's take our horses for a trot!"

It was warm the day Father and Marcus set forth on their first trip to collect supplies for the Patriots. Felicity and Ben stood in the doorway of the store, waving good-bye. Felicity felt proud. Father looked handsome and strong, and Penny's coat shone bright as gold in the sunshine. *Good-bye,* she thought as Penny and Father and Marcus disappeared down the dusty, crowded street. *Come back safely, all of you.*

When she could not see them anymore, Felicity turned and followed Ben into the store. She stood as tall as she could behind the counter. Very soon the door opened, and her first customer came in.

"Good day, Miss Merriman!" the customer said. It was Elizabeth.

"Good day, Miss Cole," Felicity said with a smile. "And how may I help you today?"

LOOKING BACK
1·7·7·4

A PEEK INTO
THE PAST

*A nineteenth-century artist's idea of what a Revolutionary
War battle looked like.*

The Revolutionary War not only changed thirteen
English colonies into the United States of America—it
also changed the city of Williamsburg and the daily
lives of families like Felicity's. Before the war,
Williamsburg was a bustling center of politics, business,
and fashion. It was the capital of Virginia and the most
important city in the large colony. But when the
Patriots began the fight for independence from

*Patriots wanted everyone in the colonies, shown here as
parts of a snake, to join together to work for independence.*

JOIN OR

England, life in Williamsburg became very different.

After Governor Dunmore left Williamsburg in June 1775, angry colonists raided his Palace to take the weapons that were stored

The entrance hall of the Governor's Palace, where weapons were arranged on the ceiling and walls.

there. A few days later, Patriot troops raided the Governor's Palace again. Some of them moved into the building and made it their camp. Soldiers took over other parts of Williamsburg, too. Soon more than 2,000 men were camping out there, waiting for supplies and instructions before leaving for the battlefront. Residents like Felicity saw signs of the war everywhere as they walked down the city streets.

Life also changed for Loyalist families. Families like Elizabeth's were often separated. Loyalist men could be arrested for supporting the king, just as Mr. Cole was.

The parts of the snake are labeled with the first letters of the colonies. "NE" stands for New England.

Women and children worked hard to keep their homes and farms running while men were off at battle.

So, many men went back to England or to places like New York City that had been captured by the English. Their wives and children stayed in Williamsburg to protect their homes and property from colonists who were angry at them for being loyal to the king.

Patriot families like Felicity's also were often separated. Husbands and older brothers went off to fight in the Revolutionary War. After they left, women like Mrs. Merriman and children like Felicity had more work to do. They continued to tend their animals and work in their gardens, and now they had to manage their families' households and businesses, too. There was also more work because many male slaves left to join the army. Yet as busy as women and children were,

About 5,000 African Americans fought in the Revolutionary War. Slaves were promised freedom for their service.

they still knit stockings and caps and sewed shirts to give to soldiers in the army.

Americans made their own gunpowder during the war because England stopped selling it to the former colonies. Soldiers carried gunpowder in powder horns like this one.

People in Williamsburg could not buy all the things they could before the war. Shopkeepers had once sold many imported goods—goods brought in from England and other countries. But during the war, England stopped selling to the former colonies. And England tried to keep ships from other countries from entering American ports. So people had a hard time finding imported goods such as chocolate, coffee, tea, china, and silk.

As the war went on, people made many of the things they needed. Families drank homemade cider instead of coffee or tea. They made clothing from homespun cloth instead of imported cloth bought in a store. Like other Williamsburg women, Mrs. Merriman worried about being able to replace her children's clothing as it wore out. She used her sewing skills to take apart and remake clothing so that worn parts would not show. If

During the war, many families spun and dyed their own yarn to weave into cloth like this.

a new piece of clothing was absolutely necessary, she used homespun cloth instead of fine silk or cotton.

Families worried about the health and safety of their loved ones in the army. Mail was not delivered on a regular schedule during the war, so a letter from a soldier might take months to reach his family. People in Williamsburg and other communities shared whatever information they had about the war. Taverns, where visitors from out of town stayed, buzzed with news about the war.

Soldiers worried about the safety of their families at home as

People often shared news of the war in taverns.

well. Williamsburg lies between the James and the York rivers, and British raiders sometimes sailed up those rivers close to Williamsburg. In 1780, the capital of Virginia was moved from Williamsburg to Richmond, partly because people worried that Williamsburg might be attacked. In 1781, the last year of the war, fighting actually took place just outside Williamsburg, and residents like Felicity feared for their lives. Many American families lived near other battlegrounds and felt the same danger.

The fight for independence from England changed the lives of all Americans. Nearly everyone suffered in some way. But people like the Merrimans learned to live with the difficulties. They looked forward to being together again when the war was over, as citizens of a new nation, the United States of America.

A naval battle off the coast of Virginia in 1781.

THE AMERICAN GIRLS COLLECTION®

There are more books in The American Girls Collection. They're filled with the adventures that four lively American girls—Felicity, Kirsten, Samantha, and Molly—lived long ago.

But the books are only part of The American Girls Collection—only the beginning. There are lovable dolls—Felicity, Kirsten, Samantha, and Molly dolls—that have beautiful clothes and lots of wonderful accessories. They make these stories of the past come alive today for American girls like you.

To learn about The American Girls Collection, fill out this postcard and mail it to Pleasant Company. We will send you a catalogue about all the books, dolls, dresses, and other delights in The American Girls Collection.

I'm an American girl who loves to get mail.
Please send me a catalogue of The American Girls Collection®:

My name is _____

My address is _____

City _____ State _____ Zip _____

My Birthday is _____ My age is ____

I am in ____ grade.   Parent's Signature _____

The book this postcard is in came from:
☐ a bookstore   ☐ the Pleasant Company Catalogue
☐ a library   ☐ a friend or relative

If the postcard has already
been removed from this book
and you would like to receive
a Pleasant Company catalogue,
please send your name and
address to:

PLEASANT COMPANY
P.O. Box 497
Middleton, WI 53562-9940
or, call our toll-free number
1-800-845-0005